What's Up, Chuck?

Leo Landry

Charlesbridge

For Yolanda Scott and Susan Sherman

Published by Charlesbridge
85 Main Street
Watertown, MA 02472
(617) 926-0329
www.charlesbridge.com

Library of Congress Cataloging-in-Publication Data
Landry, Leo, author.
What's Up, Chuck?/Leo Landry.
pages cm
Summary: Chuck the woodchuck is a skilled sculptor in wood,
and he has won the Best of the Forest art contest three years in a row,
but this year he faces a serious challenge from a newcomer, Scooter Possum.
ISBN 978-1-58089-698-6 (reinforced for library use)
ISBN 978-1-60734-914-3 (ebook)
ISBN 978-1-60734-915-0 (ebook pdf)
1. Woodchuck—Juvenile fiction. 2. Opossums—Juvenile fiction. 3. Forest
animals—Juvenile fiction. 4. Artists—Juvenile fiction. 5. Competition
(Psychology)—Juvenile Fiction. [1.Woodchuck—Fiction. 2. Opossums—
Fiction. 3. Forest animals—Fiction. 4. Artists—Fiction. 5. Competition
(Psychology)—Fiction.] I. Title. II. Title: What's Up, Chuck?
pz7.l2317357wh 2016
813.6—dc23
[Fic]
2014049186

Printed in China
(hc) 10 9 8 7 6 5 4 3 2 1

Illustrations done in pencil and watercolor on Fabriano watercolor paper
Display type and text type set in Palatino Informal Sans
Color separations by Colourscan Print Co Pte Ltd, Singapore
Printed by 1010 Printing International Limited in Huizhou, Guangdong, China
Production supervision by Brian G. Walker
Designed by Susan Mallory Sherman

Contents

-1-
An Artist

Chuck was an artist. He loved to make things out of wood. He spent most of his days gnawing, sawing, sanding, and carving deep in his burrow.

"Knock, knock," said a cheery voice through the door one day.

"Who's there?" replied Chuck.

"Stopwatch," said the voice.

"Stopwatch who?" asked Chuck.

"Stopwatch you're doing and let me in!" replied the voice.

Chuck burst out laughing. "Come on in, Bear."

"What's up, Chuck?" Bear asked.

"This is my newest sculpture," answered Chuck. "I call it *Look Before You Leap*."

"Wow!" said Bear. He stepped back to admire it. "You really are the finest artist in the woods."

"Thanks, Bear," replied Chuck. "You know I love my work. Now if you'll excuse me, I need to finish this piece for the Best of the Forest art contest. I've been working on it all month."

"Good luck, Chuck," Bear said. "I bet
you'll win first prize."

-2-
The New Guy

The Forest Flier pulled into the train station with a squeal of its brakes.

"Five fifteen! Woodland Forest!" shouted the conductor.

A lone possum exited the train, walking down the Forest Flier's steel steps. He made his way to the information booth.

"Hi there," said the possum. "My name is Scooter. Scooter Possum, from Swampy Swamp. Is there somewhere an artist might stay for a few days?" he asked. "I'm preparing for the Best of the Forest art contest."

"Welcome, Scooter," said the fox on duty. "I'm Tawny. I know just the place. Let me call my friend Chuck."

Chuck answered the phone. He agreed to loan his extra room to the new possum in town.

Before long the doorbell rang.

"Come on down!" Chuck called. "You must be Scooter," the woodchuck said, offering a friendly paw. "I'm Chuck. Welcome to my burrow."

Scooter shook Chuck's paw. "What a great place you have here. And what a terrific sculpture," he said, eyeing Chuck's *Look Before You Leap*.

"Thanks," Chuck replied. He liked the possum immediately.

"Tell me, Scooter," asked Chuck at dinner that night, "what kind of art do you make?"

"Ooh, I love to paint," Scooter answered dreamily. "I gather my own paint pigments from all over Swampy Swamp. A little crushed boysenberry makes a fine purple color. Mashed buttercups make a lovely yellow. And of course there are greens everywhere. . . ."

"It sounds like you love to paint as much as I love

to carve wood," said Chuck. "Give me a freshly cut log, and I can't wait to sink my chompers into it."

"Yup. Just like I can't wait to get my paws in paint!" replied Scooter.

"We can get to work in the morning. And I've planned a welcome lunch for you. I want you to meet everyone in Woodland Forest," said Chuck.

"That's so nice of you, Chuck," said Scooter.

-3-
Work

The next morning Chuck happily put the finishing touches on his sculpture. He gnawed, sanded, and polished every last detail.

Scooter spread a large drop cloth on the floor. He then unrolled a huge canvas full of color.

"My work in progress," explained Scooter. "It's almost finished!"

The possum prepared his paints. He took out several paintbrushes. Grabbing three in each paw, Scooter dipped each brush into a different color.

"Watch," Scooter quietly suggested.

He drew both his arms back. With a quick flick of his wrists he splattered the canvas with paint from the six brushes. The color ran across the canvas, mixing together.

"There!" he declared. He dabbed one of the brushes back into the paint and flicked the brush again. "*Now* it's finished."

Chuck looked over at Scooter. "How do you know?" he gasped.

"I just get a feeling. I think I'll call this painting *Splatter Matters*. What do you think, Chuck?" Scooter asked. He picked up the canvas and pinned it to the wall.

Chuck didn't know what to say.

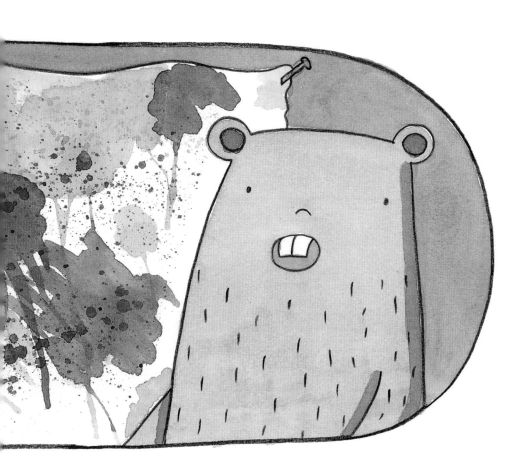

Paint was still dripping onto the drop cloth. But the painting was beautiful. The colors reminded him of a rainy spring day, when the forest was fresh and new.

"Wow," said Chuck. "*Splatter Matters*. It's lovely!"

It *is* lovely, Chuck thought. Scooter was good. *Really* good.

-4-
Lunch

Ding! Ding! Chuck tapped his spoon against his water glass.

"Thank you for coming to meet my new friend, Scooter. He's an artist, too. To celebrate, I brought everyone's favorite homemade dessert—Chuck Wood's forest-famous sweet-potato pie!"

"Hooray!" shouted the guests.

Soon everyone was eating, drinking, and telling stories about life in Woodland Forest. Scooter shared stories about Swampy Swamp. When everyone was ready for dessert, Scooter stood.

"And now for another treat," he announced. "I made *my* dessert specialty—Swampy Swamp snickerdoodles. I hope you like them."

With a flourish he presented a platter of perfectly round cookies.

"Whoa!" exclaimed the lunch guests.

"They're beautiful!" gasped Fawn. "And they smell amazing."

"*Hmpf*," grunted Chuck. "Would somebody *please* pass the sweet-potato pie?"

-5-
The Contest

It was the morning of the art contest. A crowd of Woodland Forest art lovers was admiring the entries.

"Look at all this amazing artwork," said Scooter. "Everyone is so talented."

"It's like this every year," said Chuck. "I can't believe I've won first prize three years in a row."

"You WHAT?" exclaimed Scooter. "Chuck, that's impressive."

"Thank you, thank you," replied Chuck. He took a little bow and chuckled. "Let's get back to our places. The judge will come by any minute now."

The judge, a large moose named Bull, stopped at Chuck's *Look Before You Leap* sculpture first.

"A marvel of fine-toothed carving," commented the moose. "And a 'leap' in artistic talent!"

The judge then walked over to Scooter's painting. He seemed excited. Chuck fidgeted nervously.

Soon Bull walked to the stage, stepped up to the microphone, and spoke.

"I was up to my antlers in excellent entries, but I have made my decision," he said. The crowd cheered.

"I am happy to award third prize to Shirley Squirrel for her photograph, *Tough Nut to Crack*. Congratulations!" the moose declared.

"You go, Squir'l!" yelled someone in the crowd.

"Woo-hoo!" Shirley cried, jumping up with delight. "I did it! Thanks, everyone!"

"And now . . . ," announced Bull, "the moment you've been waiting for."

"Here it comes," whispered Chuck.

27

"Second prize goes to Chuck Wood for his magnificent piece, *Look Before You Leap*. That means first prize has been won by our fine new friend, Scooter Possum. His bold painting, *Splatter Matters*, is simple yet brilliant. Congratulations to you both!"

The crowd burst into applause, and Scooter proudly made his way to the stage behind Shirley.

Meanwhile, Chuck had vanished.

6

Meltdown

Chuck was furious. He paced around his burrow and kicked his tools angrily.

"*Splatter Matters*," he growled to himself through clenched teeth. "*Splatter Matters*! UGH!"

He picked up a small sculpture called *Free as a Bird* and threw it to the floor. *SMASH!*

"Why did I ever think that I was any good?" he shouted. "The only reason I won first prize before is because there wasn't a real artist in Woodland Forest! Not until Scooter came!"

A tear slowly rolled down Chuck's cheek.

"Anybody home?" asked a chirping voice from outside Chuck's door.

"There's nobody here. Go away!" answered Chuck.

"Knock, knock."

"Ugh! Who's there?" answered Chuck.

"Lettuce," said the voice.

"Lettuce who?" answered Chuck impatiently.

"Lettuce in! It's cold out here," the voice said.

"Hardy-har-har," said Chuck, opening the door. Emmy and Fawn smiled at him.

"What's up, Chuck?" asked Emmy. "What happened? You just won second prize!"

"That says it all, doesn't it?" answered Chuck. "Second prize. Big deal. Why don't you go congratulate Scooter? He's a much better artist than I am. And he makes better desserts!"

"Listen, Chuck," said Fawn. "Second prize *is* a big deal. Congratulations!"

"And sure, Scooter is a fine artist and a swell baker," said Emmy. "But so are you, Chuck. You couldn't have won the contest three years in a row if you weren't talented."

"Whatever," said Chuck. "It doesn't matter. Only *splatter* matters." Chuck sighed.

"No," said Fawn. "What matters is that you love making art. And Scooter is your friend, remember?"

Chuck sighed again.

7

Back on Track

Chuck looked at the rubble beneath his feet. Had he really smashed his own sculpture? He decided to go for a walk to clear his head. He soon found himself at the train station.

Inside was his sculpture *Keep on Track*. He remembered how much fun it had been to carve. He had really made that wood look like it was moving!

Chuck heard a noise behind him.

"Why, hello, Chuck," said Bear. "I was just passing the station. I decided to pop in to have a look at *Keep on Track* before I delivered your trophy. It's my favorite of your sculptures."

"Thanks," Chuck replied quietly, staring at the second-place trophy.

He thought about Shirley Squirrel and how excited she had been to win third prize.

"I remember visiting while you were carving it," Bear continued. "You were still carving away when I came back in the morning."

"I loved working on it so much that I stayed up all night," Chuck said, laughing.

"You really do love what you do," Bear pointed out.
"I *do* love carving," Chuck said. "I love all of it—
the drawing, the planning, the gnawing. . . ."

"Then let's put this trophy where it belongs—in your burrow next to the ones you won before," Bear said.

"Okay, Bear," said Chuck. "It's time I got 'back on track.' And I think I owe some congratulations to my friend Scooter."

EP ON TRACK"

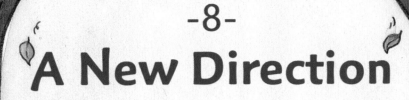

-8-
A New Direction

Scooter arrived at Chuck's burrow just as Chuck and Bear walked up.

"Hi, Chuck! Where did you go? We missed you at the Best of the Forest party," said Scooter. "Everyone wanted to get a picture of you, me, and Shirley Squirrel."

"Oh, er, I thought I had left the oven on, so I ran back to check," replied Chuck, embarrassed.

"Oh, no! Was everything okay?" Scooter cried.

"Actually, that's not true," Chuck confessed. "I was upset that you won first prize instead of me."

Scooter looked puzzled.

"But now I realize that you deserve first prize," Chuck continued. "You're my friend, and I love making my art. Awards are just whipped cream on a sweet-potato pie. Congratulations, Scooter," Chuck said, smiling.

"Thanks, Chuck. Now let's go back and get a picture with Shirley," Scooter said. "First, second, or third, we're all the 'Best of the Forest.'"

The next morning Chuck got right to work.

"Ooh—now *this* is interesting," said Chuck as he arranged the broken pieces of *Free as a Bird*.

He looked at his second-place trophy. *Not bad after all*, he thought, taking it off the shelf.

In walked Scooter. "What's up, Chuck?"

"Hi there, pal," said Chuck. "Ready for another day of art?"

"You bet!" answered Scooter. "Let's go!"

Later, Chuck admired his new sculpture. "I think I'm taking my work in a new direction," he said with a smile.

"That's great," said Scooter, looking at the rearranged carving. "What's the new name?"

"I call it *Lesson Learned*," answered Chuck.